DALMATIANS
RAINBOW PUPPIES

Written by Barbara Bazaldua
Illustrated by Len Smith and Cindi Bothner

🌟 A GOLDEN BOOK · NEW YORK

Golden Books Publishing Company, Inc., New York, New York 10106

he night before Easter, ninety-nine Dalmatian puppies
had a hard time falling asleep. It was their very first Easter,
and they were very excited. All night long they dreamed of
chocolate bunnies and colored eggs.

The next morning, the puppies got up early and ran to wake their parents, Pongo and Perdita.

"Please, may we have our very own Easter egg hunt?" they begged. "It would be so much fun!"

Pongo and Perdita looked at each other.

"All right," Perdita said. "Nanny will dye some eggs, and then we'll hide them for you."

"Hurray!" the puppies shouted, scampering into the kitchen. Eagerly they watched Nanny set out bowls of pink, blue, green, purple, and yellow dye.

Afterward, she took a basket and hurried
out to the henhouse to gather eggs.

The puppies just couldn't sit still.

"I know I'm going to find a million Easter eggs," Penny shouted, running around the kitchen.

"I'm going to find a trillion, JILLION!" Patch yelled, racing after her.

The puppies didn't see Nanny as she came in the door. Penny raced right into her. Patch slid right into Penny.

CRASH! Down went Nanny. *CRACK, SPLAT!* went the eggs.

Patch covered his eyes. Penny was too shocked to speak.
"It was just an accident, puppies," Nanny said kindly as
she cleaned up the mess. "But sit quietly this time while I
get some more eggs."

The puppies tried to hold still—they really did. But Rolly wanted to get a closer look at the bowls of dye, so he climbed up on the table.

"Hey, I can see my reflection!" he said. "I look all purple!"

"Let me see," said Penny. As she put her paws on the table to climb up, she bumped Rolly. Oops! Into the purple dye went his nose!

"Your nose looks like a grape!" Patch said, giggling.

"You look so funny!" Penny said, landing next to Rolly. And—oops!—into the green dye went her left paw!

"Uh-oh!" she said, trying to shake the dye off. Drops of green dye sailed through the air and settled on the puppies.

As Rolly backed away from the flying drops, he knocked over the pink dye. It hit the floor, splattering his brothers and sisters with pink raindrops.

"Hey! This is fun!" shouted Patch, jumping onto the table. With one paw he began to splash yellow dye all over the puppies, and with the other he sprinkled them with blue.

Finally, all the puppies joined in the fun. Soon, every single one of them was covered with spots in every color of the rainbow. The kitchen looked very colorful, too.

Suddenly, Lucky heard Nanny returning. He looked at his brothers and sisters. Then he looked at the kitchen.

"Uh-oh," he said. "Nanny isn't going to like this.
We'd better find someplace to hide."

The puppies raced outside.
Penny ducked behind the henhouse.
Patch and Rolly curled up in the flower bed.

Lucky crawled under a garden basket.
There were puppies hiding under every bush,
behind every rock, and in the tall grass.

"Oh, my!" Nanny exclaimed loudly when she came into the kitchen.

Roger, Anita, Pongo, and Perdita came running to see what had happened.

"Where did the puppies go?" Anita asked.
"I think I know," Nanny replied, pointing to a trail of colored paw prints.

Roger, Anita, Pongo, Perdita, and Nanny followed the paw prints, first to the henhouse, then to the flower bed, the garden basket, and to every place the colorful trail led.

When they saw all ninety-nine rainbow-spotted pups, Roger and Anita laughed and laughed, and the others soon joined in.

"Why, you puppies match the Easter surprises I bought for you," Nanny exclaimed, wiping tears of laughter from her eyes.

She bustled into the house and came back with a big basket of ribbons.

"I bought Easter ribbons for your collars," she said. "Now your spots and your ribbons match!"

Roger and Anita helped Nanny tie ninety-nine ribbons on ninety-nine colorful puppies. There were ribbons for Pongo and Perdita, too.

Then all one hundred one Dalmatians sat proudly for a family photograph.

"We were planning an Easter egg hunt," Nanny said, smiling. "But it looks like we had an Easter pup hunt, instead!"